LOOPS

LOOPS

Poems by

Toni Stern

CIRCLESTAR

SANTA BARBARA

Published in the United Sates
by Circle Star Press.
Santa Barbara, California

Library of Congress Cataloging-in-Publication Data

Stern, Toni
Loops
Poems
1. Title
ISBN 978-0-578-78650-6

Printed in the United States of America
10 9 8 7 6 5 4 3 2 1

Cover design by John Balkwill and Trish Reynales
Cover photo by Jerry Rounds
Back cover photo of Toni Stern by Cheryl Finnegan
Book design by Lumino Press

This book is for my mother

And he was told but these few words that opened up his heart—if you cannot bring good news then don't bring any.

—Bob Dylan, "Wicked Messenger"

Sane people did what their neighbors did, so if there were any lunatics at large, one might know how to avoid them.

—George Eliot, *Middlemarch*

CONTENTS

I

The Way Back 17

Mystery Box 18

Loops 19

All That Glitters 20

Big Business 21

You Never Know 22

Funny Man 23

Seadog 24

Merry Go Round 25

Dealing with Loss 26

Seven A.M. 27

Stairway to the Stars 28

Splash 29

Planetary Protection Officer 30

End of Story 31

Let's Make It Interesting 32

Cavalier On Horseback Bearing Flowers 33

Extraordinary Measures 34

Episodes 35

New Wave 36

Application 37

Playing with Fire 38

San Francisco Bay Blues 39

Preparations 40

What Could Go Wrong 41

II

The Great Outdoors 45

Heartland 46

Snapshot 47

Over the Holidays 48

The Cosmatron 49

Mother's Day 50

Love Is Strange 51

Time Has Wings 52

Breathing Room 53

Hostages 54

Providence 55

High Fidelity 56

Departure 57

Curbed 58

Utopia 59

Ruffle 60

Entrepreneurs 61

Readymade 62

Unanimous 63

III

Late Summer 67

Sandwich 68

Covey 69

A Wonderful Life 70

Roots 71

The Economist 72

Last Word 73

I Forgive You 74

Sleeping Tiger 75

Cliffhanger 76

Prodigal Son 77

The Family Jewels 78

Cellar Door 79

Almost True Story 80

So Close 81

Tailspin 82

Lover Boy 83

Crickets 84

The Secret of Life 85

More Light 86

Jump 87

Chair 88

Solitaire 89

Self Reliance 90

Pressure Drop 91

Twenty Four Karat 92

99 Ways 93

The Way Back

I was lying by the fire when I heard footsteps. "Who goes there?" I said. An enormous birdlike creature approached. "Don't come any closer," I said. "You're in my cave," the creature said. "You abandoned it," I said. "Besides, I've made improvements." "It smells terrible in here," the creature said, thrusting its beak inside the entrance. I grabbed my axe and started swinging. The creature retreated—very nimbly, I thought, given its size. "The others will be arriving soon," the creature said. "I have nowhere else to go," I said. "We don't feed on whatever it is you're made of," the creature said, "we just need a place to live."

Mystery Box

A large box is delivered to the house. I expect it to be heavy when I pick it up, but it weighs less than three pounds. The first thing that comes to mind is tarantulas: a box of tarantulas. I'm not afraid of spiders, but the idea of a box of tarantulas unnerves me. I go to the kitchen and make myself a cup of tea. Perhaps it's a hand-painted scarf, sent by an admirer. Perhaps it's a bird's nest, a single rose, or a beach pebble. Maybe it's a government bond, a summons, or an amputated finger. I use my foot to slide the mystery box next to the couch, unplug the table lamp from my nightstand, place the lamp on top of the box, and open the apocalyptic thriller I've been reading. It'll take my mind off things.

Loops

A man I didn't recognize stopped me on the street. "Excuse me," he said. "You're wearing my hat." Since I wasn't wearing a hat, his remark struck me as odd, but I played along. "That's impossible," I said, "I've had this hat for years." "I can understand why you'd say that," he said, "but that doesn't alter the facts." "I would never wear someone else's hat," I said, "It would be like wearing someone else's, I don't know, someone else's socks." "You needn't be vulgar," he said. "I'm sorry you feel that way," I said. "I didn't mean to offend you." "Keep the hat if it means that much to you," he said. "It looks better on you anyway."

All That Glitters

We were anchored leeward, a half mile off Pelican Island,
when an enormous wave struck our sailboat. It snapped
the mast, swamped the deck, and flooded the cockpit.
The captain, a hand surgeon and weekend sailor, my
boyfriend, his sister, and I found ourselves hopelessly
ill-prepared for real weather. The boat, already listing,
began to sink. The unsecured dinghy pitched over
the side, as did the life jackets. With great effort we
scrambled up the starboard bow and hung on for dear
life. Sometime after sunset the Coast Guard arrived.
"Sticks out like a sore thumb," my boyfriend joked,
indicating the half-submerged wreck, from the safety of
our recovery vessel. "The sea wants to kill you," my dad
said, when he met us at the harbor. "Now you know."

Big Business

Marley works across the street from me in Midtown. When we can, we like to walk to the subway together. This afternoon she looked completely worn out. "What a dreadful day," she said. "The FBI raided our offices and interrogated upper-level management for over five hours." "What were they looking for?" I said. "I have no idea," she said. "We're a yogurt company." "Maybe your boss is a mobster," I said. "Mr. Ellingsworth?" she said. "He's the gentlest man I ever met. As senior vice-president of Yak Yogurt, I'd know if there was anything illegal going on." "Did the Feds question you?" I said. "Did they ever," she said. "They made me feel like a criminal." "You look like you could use a drink," I said. "You're not afraid to be seen with me?" she said. "Don't be silly," I said. She slipped her arm through mine, and for the first time ever—I felt as if I were being watched.

You Never Know

I fly to Las Vegas on the red-eye out of Santa Marina.
I've played a little poker in my day, and I'm feeling
lucky. I check into The Silver Spur, change my shirt,
and hit the tables. A waitress comes over and I order a
Scotch. "It's on the house," she says. Before I've finished
the first one, the waitress brings me another, then
another, then another after that, "on the house." I'm a
fireman, accustomed to stressful situations, but nothing's
prepared me for this. I wake up in an alley. My shoelaces,
wallet, and two teeth are missing. I can't find my car.
Someone's stuffed a bus ticket in my pocket, along with
a note: "Thanks for a wonderful evening." When I return
to work on Monday, the captain asks if I'd had any luck.
"You should have been there," I say. "I was on fire."

FUNNY MAN

A guy who'd been hanging around the club stumbles
over to our table while the fellas and I kick back at
the Blue Spot. "Are you a comedienne?" he says,
addressing me. "Why, yes I am," I say, mildly flattered.
"Say something funny," he says. "Artichoke hearts,"
I say. "That's not funny," he says. "Maybe if I'd had
a little more time," I say. "You're not one of those
improvisational types are you," he says, dragging
out the word. "Nope," I say. "Not one of those. You
should stick around, catch my act." He gives me a
boozy, conspiratorial grin. "Are you flirting with me?"
he says. "I don't think so," I say. "No one flirts with
me anymore," he says, gloomily, "that's why I drink."
"Hilarious," I say. "Can I use it?"

Seadog

In my previous life I was a dog. Not just any dog, mind you. In 1845, I was a member of the spectacularly ill-fated quest for the Northwest Passage, led by Rear-Admiral Sir John Franklin. We all perished: me, the cat, the little capuchin I was so fond of, and of course the two great ships' entire crew. I won't burden you with the calamities we faced and ultimately succumbed to in that ice-encased wilderness, except to say that it was heartbreaking. Now, after all these years, having been reincarnated as a Dane, I feel somehow compensated for my previous travails. Life is good, food and shelter plentiful, and I live, for the most part, untroubled and content. Do I believe in cosmic justice? Not at all. *Jeg er bare en heldig pige.* I'm just a lucky girl.

MERRY GO ROUND

I was cutting through the park when I ran into Helena, my old flame. She was as lovely as ever and I told her so. Helena put her fingers to her lips. "You can't speak?" I said. She nodded. "Have you taken a vow of silence?" I said. Helena rolled her eyes. "Are you ill?" "No," she said, by way of a head shake. "What is it then?" I said. Helena shrugged. I bought a couple of sodas and we strolled in amicable silence. Helena was drawn to the park's main attraction by the hearty boom of its calliope. She beamed and tugged at my arm. "I'd get too dizzy," I said. "You go." Helena climbed aboard a jewel-encrusted horse and the carousel came to life. Helena waved as she flew by, but when I attempted to wave back, my knees buckled and I collapsed. "Are you alright?" a voice said. "Helena?" I said. "I thought that was you," she said. "No," I said, my head swimming, "it's you. It's always been you."

Dealing With Loss

"I should have won," Bianca said, when I ran into her after the ceremony. "That should have been me up there." "It's a travesty," I said. "And this is how they repay me," she said. "I've half a mind to unmask this gaudy farce." "You've endured so much," I said. "Why don't you sleep on it." Bianca dug her nails into my forearm. "*You* still love me, don't you?" she said. "Of course I do," I said. "We all do." "You're sweet," she said. "Who are you again?"

Seven a.m.

I wake to the sound of Pepito's nails, tap-tapping on
the hardwood floor. "Good morning, Carol," he says,
dancing around my legs as I shuffle to the kitchen.
"What's for breakfast?" "Wait a minute," I say, opening
the fridge, "when did you start talking?" "Oh, Carol,"
he says, "I've been asking you the same question for
years." "How come I never noticed?" I say. "Never
mind that," Pepito says, "focus, Carol, focus." Just then,
Trilby, our obese cat, squeezes through the doggie
door. "What a night," she says. "I could eat a horse." A
moment later, my husband, still in his pajamas, trots
in with the morning paper. "Woof," he says. "This is
crazy," I say. I back out of the kitchen and race down
the hall. Pepito, hot on my heels, follows me into the
bedroom. "Go away!" I say. "What are you doing under
there, Carol?" Pepito says, lifting the bed skirt with his
nose. "You know the rules—no playing hide-and-seek
until after breakfast."

Stairway to the Stars

Teddy parked the car next to the trailhead, and we hiked up to the observatory. From there, we had a bird's eye view of Los Angeles. Night was falling, and we held hands as the streetlights came on. "Pretty soon the stars will be out," Teddy said, drawing me closer. Suddenly, a film crew rushed onto the observation deck. "You're in the shot," someone shouted. "Move it!"

Splash

"I could spend the entire day sharing my wit and aspirations with you," Loretta said, "but this novel isn't going to write itself." "How's your heroine?" I said. "Her limp is barely perceptible," Loretta said, "but the emotional scars run deep." "And the climate scientist?" I said. "Turns out he was a red herring," she said. "Uncle Rodrigo has no alibi for the evening in question, and the lead detective might know more than he's saying—I haven't a clue where this is going." "It'll come," I said. "You see this?" Loretta said, flipping her shoulder-length curls. "It's a wig—hair loss due to stress. I'm tempted to put all my characters in a room together and liquefy the lot of them. *Kaboom*."

PLANETARY PROTECTION OFFICER

I take my job as Planetary Protection Officer seriously.
Earth is my current orbit. After twelve hundred years
on Saturn, and nine hundred on Uranus, I've received
a "promotion." Talk about culture shock! My first
assignment was to assess, within three one hundred
thousandths of a percent, the ratio of ants to humans at
any given moment; a calculation any human could easily
perform. Though it's an impressive number: one billion,
six hundred and seventy-two million, five hundred and
eighty-four thousand and seven to one, my report clearly
states there's no cause for alarm. Even so, they go on and
on about the ants. I hope Mom and Dada are receiving
my transmissions. I miss them. For all its beauty, Earth is
a lonely place.

END OF STORY

"I just came from upstairs," Monique said. "I heard Proctor telling his followers we're to be terminated." "Why?" Annabella said. "We've done everything they've asked." "Sold our souls and sealed our fate," Jackson said. "What about the children?" Annabella cried. "Get ahold of yourself," Elder warned. "We will behave as if nothing is amiss, then, when they least suspect it, make our escape. Agreed?" The mice, unaccustomed to making decisions, faltered. "Agreed," Monique said finally. Annabella, her dark eyes moist, nodded her assent. "Agreed," Jackson said. "Speak up," Elder said, pressing the others. "Cat got your—" The basement door burst open. "Okay, boys," Proctor said, "they're all yours."

"Remind me again," I said. "Is it god or the devil who's in the details?" "Funny you should ask," Mo said. "I've been pondering that very question myself." "And?" I said. "That's the thing," Mo said. "I can't make up my mind one way or the other—and I'm usually a very decisive person." "I suppose we could look it up," I said. "We could," Mo said, "but who can you trust?" "Good point," I said. "Do we know who won the game tonight?" "It's probably in the final minutes," Mo said. "Shall I turn it on?" "My money's on the home team," I said. "Okay, then," Mo said, "I'll take the visitors."

Cavalier on Horseback Bearing Flowers

"I'm writing a screenplay," I said. "What's it called?"
Virginia said. "Cavalier on Horseback Bearing Flowers,"
I said. "What's it about?" she said. "It's about a
melancholy man who divests himself of everything he's
ever owned—everything connected to his past." "And
then?" Virginia said. "Then he buys a one-way ticket to
the end of the line," I said. "What does he do when he
gets there?" she said. "He searches for love," I said. "Does
he find it?" she said. "I don't know," I said. "I haven't
gotten that far." "I hope there's a horse in the story," she
said. "So do I," I said.

Extraordinary Measures

"What happened?" Amy said, when I hobbled into the bakery. She came around the counter and guided me to a seat. "I lost control of my car driving up the coast," I said, handing her my crutches. "It spun out, jumped the guard rail, and plunged three hundred feet onto the rocks. For a week I survived off rainwater and a bag of pine nuts, until a fishing boat spotted the wreck and radioed for help. I just got out of the hospital this morning." "That's terrible," Amy said. "It was all over the news." I said. "I'm so sorry, Roger," she said. "I've been in Mexico all month. My cousin was arrested for public intoxication in Michoacán, and the cops want ten thousand dollars for her release. I keep telling them we don't have that kind of money, but they think all Americans are rich." "Which cousin?" I said. "The pretty one," she said. "Rosalind?" I said. Amy smiled. "What now?" I said. "I have to convince them we can't afford to pay that much," she said. "How's your Spanish?" I said. "*Muy malo*," she said. I felt a sharp pain in my hip. "I have to keep moving or my body shuts down," I said, struggling to my feet. "Don't worry, Amy," I said, "you'll dig your way out of this." Amy's face brightened. "It's a crazy idea," she said, "but it just might work."

Episodes

I learned that Cousin Peg was in trouble from Aunt
Mary. Family first I told myself and drove for eleven
hours. Aunt Mary met me at the front door. "How is
she," I said. When Peg heard my voice, she stomped
into the living room. She'd grown enormous—her eyes,
barely discernible in her fleshy face. "Zadie!" she said,
dragging me into her nightmare. "You're just in time."
She picked me up and carried me to the curb. "Get in,"
she said, opening the passenger door. "Where are we
going?" I said. "Keys," she said, holding out her hand.
We drove to the industrial part of town, abandoned now
for decades. "Let's get to work," she said, retrieving a tire
iron from the trunk. "Is this a game?" I said, trudging
after her. "Here" she said, stripping off her blue and
yellow dishwashing gloves, "put these on." Peg pulled
a rusty revolver from her back pocket and kissed the
barrel. "Is that a real gun?" I said. We combed the filthy
warehouses until dawn. "What now?" I said, swatting the
cobwebs ensnared in my hair. "You look ridiculous," Peg
said. "Coffee?"

New Wave

Jan was sitting on the edge of the couch, attempting to steady the cup of tea I'd just brought her. "You realize there's no such thing as zombies," I said. "You wouldn't say that if you met the woman in 3B," she said. "I just pray I can stay on the right side of her. If anything happens to me, if I disappear or something, tell the police what you know." "Do you think she wants to suck your blood?" I said. "That's vampires," she said. "Vampires suck your blood, werewolves tear you to shreds. Zombies eat you." "What makes you think she's a zombie?" I said. "Not only her," Jan said. "Her husband's a zombie, too—but I'm not afraid of him. He has a thing for me. If his wife finds out, though...." "More tea?" I said. "Where do they come from anyway?" she said. "The undead?" I said. Jan shuddered. "The previous tenants were French-Canadian," she said. "I never had any problems with them."

APPLICATION

"How would you describe yourself?" the interviewer said. "Broke," I said. "Do you consider yourself a *watcher,* a *sleeper,* or a *dreamer*?" the interviewer said. "What?" I said. "Which century do you think was the most fun?" the interviewer said. "This job," I said, "it's part-time, right?" "Is it better to get what you want, or want what you get?" the interviewer said. "I need the work," I said. "Do you believe discretion is the better part of dinner?" he said. "Yes?" I said. "Are you able to forgive and forget?" the interviewer said. "I could try," I said. "But it's highly unlikely."

Playing with Fire

Portia said, "Not only are all men not created equal, they never were, nor shall they ever be—and as for inalienable rights? Please." "Whoa," I said. "I've had it easy," she went on, "but the endless suffering and misery, both endured and unendurable, is ironclad evidence of disinterestedness on a cosmic scale." "I take it then, you don't believe in God," I said. "I didn't say that," said Portia.

San Francisco Bay Blues

For eighteen anguished months I've been aboard the USS *Cole*, assigned, conscripted really, to serve my beleaguered country. I'm a war correspondent, have been for decades. But this! California's succession has convulsed the nation. As if things weren't bad enough, it's rumored the former governor, now president of California, has been in closed-door discussions with the premier of Mexico. I'm a native Californian—went to UC Santa Cruz, interned at the *East Bay Times*. I surfed. Though my family and I were priced out years ago, we are forever where we came from. The USS *Cole*, stationed just outside San Francisco Bay, is what the Navy calls a destroyer. She, along with several other warships, superintend the California coast—ominous, unrelenting, and tragic. My daily dispatches are little more than stammerings; the mood aboard ship, funereal. We are adrift.

PREPARATIONS

"Hey, Carl," Billie says, "what can I do you for?" I've known Billie since grade school. Even then he wanted to be a pharmacist. "I can't sleep," I tell him. "You're not the only one," he says. "Folks around here have been losing sleep ever since the lights appeared." "What lights?" I say. "Good grief, Carl," he says. "The lights that have been tearing across the night sky for the past month." "I thought they were shooting stars," I say. "They're definitely not stars," Billie says. "I just need something to help me sleep," I say. "My friend," he says, "I'm a pharmacist, not a magician. We're going to have to let this phenomenon play itself out. Meanwhile, keep your shades drawn, your doors locked, and pray your wife and family will be spared."

What Could Go Wrong

"There's a federally funded program for that," Julian said, when I told him I was considering relinquishing my citizenship. "It's called Opt Out. Two of my coworkers have used it." "Were they satisfied with the service?" I said. "That's the thing," Julian said. "They told me they'd write as soon as they were resettled, but I haven't heard a word from either of them." "Do you think something's happened?" I said. "I'm hoping it just means they're really busy," he said. "It's probably nothing," I said. "If you do decide to leave the country," Julian said, "be sure to keep in touch." "You can count on me," I said.

II

THE GREAT OUTDOORS

When, after missing for four days, Sal was found, barely
breathing and severely sunburned, Marie, Sal's wife,
agonized over what to tell their girls. "Where's Daddy?"
they kept asking. A policewoman arrived and offered
to drive Marie to the hospital. Sal's parents, who'd
flown in the previous day, volunteered to watch the
children. "Who wants to go swimming?" Sal's mother
said, mustering a smile. "We do, we do!" they said. "He's
dehydrated and disoriented," the doctor said. "He'll sleep
tonight, but tomorrow he'll be in a lot of pain." "What
could have possessed him," Marie said, "wandering
into the desert like that." "Do you think your husband
may have been suicidal?" the doctor said. "Who do you
think you are, Sal?" Marie said, when she returned to
the hospital the next day. "Indiana Jones?" "I'm Indiana
Jones!" Sal said, attempting to sit up. "Easy does it,
professor," Marie said. "You're needed here."

Heartland

Flo got up later than usual. She'd slept badly. Bloodthirsty pythons and homicidal balloons ambushed her dreams. She lay in bed an extra moment, wondering what her husband was up to. He's probably in the kitchen, she told herself—making toast. "Ray," she said, "you still here?" When she walked into the kitchen and Ray wasn't there, she pulled on her boots. "Ray," she called. "Where are you, Ray?" The barn door was ajar, and she went in. She found him, sitting on a rickety milk stool, sobbing. "I thought you were dead," he said. "You're always up before me, but this morning you were just lying there, not moving, and I knew you were gone." "Oh, Ray," she said. "I'm a coward," Ray said. Flo knelt beside her husband, and stroked his stubbly cheek. "Come now," she said, "we'd better go feed the chickens before they fly the coop."

Snapshot

Molly came into the bedroom while Quincy was getting dressed, and sat on the edge of the bed. "I have a confession to make," she said. "This confession," he said, "is it going to make me feel better?" "Probably not," she said. "I'm not sure I want to hear it," Quincy said. "I love you," she said. "Buttering me up?" he said. "Maybe I already know what you're going to say." "Can you forgive me?" she said. "Yes," he said, "but if you do it again, I'll leave you." "I've been waiting for you to say that for so long," she said. "All this time, I never really knew if you cared or not." "Oh, I care," he said. "I wasn't taken in by the money," she said. "That crowd— it felt like slumming." "I don't want to discuss it anymore," he said. "I know," Molly said. "I want to talk about my feelings and you want to pretend you don't have any." "Classic, right?" Quincy said. "Maddening comes to mind," said Molly.

Over the Holidays

"What do you want to be when you grow up?" the
department store Santa asked Pipa. Pipa looked to her
mother for help, but her mother was looking elsewhere.
"A horse," she said. "Ho ho ho," Santa said. "A horse?
You can't grow up to be a horse. Why don't you wish for
a horse instead?" "I'm going to be a palomino horse and
run so fast no one will ever catch me," she said. "I'll live
by a lake, eat grass, and have lots of friends. I'll rescue
them from rustlers, and take care of them when they're
sick. Can I go now?" "Ho ho ho," said Santa. "What did
you ask Santa for?" her mother said, when they were in
the car. "Just stuff," Pipa said, staring out the window.
"What's wrong?" her mother said. "Nothing," Pipa said,
as she sailed over traffic, her tail barely skimming the
cooped-up cars, corralled by the Christmas crush.

THE COSMATRON

"Can you help me with this?" Dave said, indicating the object perched on his desk. "What is it?" Hal said. "Something I inherited from my father," he said. "He called it the Cosmatron." "Pretty," Hal said. "I can't figure out whether it does anything or not," Dave said. Hal picked up the Cosmatron. As he did, one of its appendages slid open. "A hidden compartment!" Dave said. He took the Cosmatron from Hal, and coaxed the yellowed paper from its recesses. "Dear son," he read. "If you've found this note, you've unlocked the mystery of the Cosmatron." "Is that it?" Hal said. "There's more," Dave said, "but the ink has faded. Except for the last line, I can't make out the words." "What's it say?" Hal said. "Love always, Dad," said Dave.

Mother's Day

No sooner had Frank walked through the door than his wife appeared from the kitchen. "Something smells good," he said. "You're a real heel," Patty said. "You're never home. In fact, you're rarely within five hundred miles of here." "Sweetheart, please," Frank said, "I'm a salesman—it's how I make my living." "There are other ways to make a living," Patty said, then added, "if you wanted to." "I swear, Patty," Frank said, "I never meant to hurt you. Truth is, I'm just not a reliable person." "You deceived me," Patty said. "Guilty as charged," he said. "If only I could lock you up," she said. "If only," said Frank.

Love is Strange

Spencer and Adele had just had a huge blowout over how to stack the dinner dishes. "I washed them," he said, "I'll stack them any way I please." I'm the one who has to put them away," Adele said. "By rights, I should get the last word as to how they're stacked." "You're impossible," her husband said. Adele was used to criticism—water off a duck's back, she called it. Growing up, little Adele tyrannized her sweet-tempered parents, and lorded over her three younger siblings. "Mind your own beeswax," "Go away," and "I hate you" were the soundtrack of her childhood. "You're mean" was another. She was horrified when her baby sister was born and she no longer had her gold and pink bedroom to herself. "From now on," she told her husband, "I'll do the dishes myself." "That's my girl," said Spencer.

Time Has Wings

"How do you prepare for a thing like that?" Carmen said. "A thing like what?" Mina said. "That," she said, pointing to their reflection in the storefront window. "We're old." "Granted," Mina said, "but we still look great in good lighting." "We do," Carmen said, "but we can't be backlit all the time." Mina laughed. "You'd look wonderful in that jacket," she said, indicating the window display. "It's definitely my color," Carmen said. "After you," Mina said, with a sweep of her arm. Nodding their appreciation to the doorman, the two friends, one petite, the other tall, animated by their newfound raison d'être, fairly waltzed into the boutique's pastel-hued embrace.

Breathing Room

Clive and Stevie were cooling their heels in one of the few remaining mountain streams flowing that late in the season. Inaccessible by vehicle, these oases were a haven—never more than now, when the lakefront was beset by tourists. "You know that commandment about love thy neighbor," Stevie said. "Why is that so difficult?" "I think we're all feeling the squeeze," Clive said. "I can't wait till winter," Stevie said. "I'm never happier than in a blizzard." "You're a rare bird," Clive said. "The weird lady in the woods," Stevie said. "Nobody calls you that," Clive said. "What do they call me?" Stevie said. "You're the woman who talks to trees," Clive said. "You're a legend."

HOSTAGES

"Aren't you the Mona Lisa?" Don Quixote said." "It's Signora Giocondo to you, bub," the woman said, taking a seat at the bar. "Martini, dry," she told the barista. "Allow me to introduce myself," the knight said. "I am Don Quixote de la Mancha, and this is my faithful squire, Sancho Panza." Sancho Panza, who'd just entered the bar, bowed. "Your humble servant," he said. "You're too modest," Signora Giocondo said, "After all, isn't Don Quixote your invention?" "Most people would say it's the other way around," Sancho Panza said. "Tell me about it," she said. "That puffed up da Vinci hijacked my life." "You were on the cover of *Mad* magazine," Sancho Panza said. "I read your book," Signora Gioconda said. "It's long." "Alas, signora, it only feels that way," said Sancho Panza. "Bartender," Signora Giocondo said, "bring this man a drink."

PROVIDENCE

"Here we are!" Natalie said. "Go on now." She gently but firmly booted both pups out of the truck and drove off. The one they called Martha was black, save for a splash of white on her chest. The male, Midnight, was all black. The pups were leftovers from a sickly litter Toyon, the family's retriever, had given birth to four months earlier. "Damn dogs," Natalie muttered. "We can barely feed ourselves, let alone a bunch of mongrels." She switched on the radio. A song she once loved spilled out of the beat-up truck's beat-up dashboard. "What am I going to tell my kids?" She found the pups exactly where she'd left them. "Get in," she ordered the ecstatic pair, "it's freezing out here."

High Fidelity

"What was that?" Fiona said, sitting straight up in bed. "What?" her husband said. The digital clock glowed 4:00 A.M. "That noise," she said. "as if the sky's being ripped apart." "It's probably just a plane," he said. "Not at this hour," she said. "All I hear is a distant rumbling," he said. "Distant rumbling?" she said. "It's deafening!" She punched him in the arm, and he stumbled to his feet. "We have to get out of here—now." Outside, frantic mothers were shoving sleepy-eyed children and clueless husbands into cars. "Which way?" he said, backing out of the driveway. "Left, left," she said. "Away from the roar." "What roar?" he said. "Oh, my God," she said. "We're doomed."

Departure

She tries reading the map, but she might as well be deciphering code. She takes Exit 168 instead of 186 and undershoots the airport by twenty miles. She hears her name, along with "final call," as she pulls into the parking garage. Inside the terminal, late to the gate, she learns that her flight is closed. A fifty-minute plane ride, if she were to continue, has just become a nine-hour drive. Forty years ago, she would have considered it an adventure. She returns to her car, pays for her brief parking privileges, and drives away.

Curbed

Fifteen-year-old Dorthea was sitting on her porch flipping through a teen magazine, when two boys from school rolled up. Jesse was driving the supercharged '69 Oldsmobile convertible he was famous for, Gary was riding shotgun. "Hey, Dorthea," Jesse said. "Wanna go for a ride?" Dorthea half-turned her head. "Dollar," she called. "Come here, boy." An enormous Great Dane appeared from the dark of the house and sat next to Dorthea. "That your boyfriend?" Jesse said. Gary snickered. The boys continued their heckling, but only Dollar appeared interested. He stood up, stretched his powerful frame, and ambled to the curb. Jesse gunned the engine—the noise from the customized mufflers drowning their final jeers as the two boys sped away. Dollar trotted back to Dorthea. "Good dog, Dollar," she said. "Good dog."

Utopia

"Mommy," Charlotte said, "is there really such a place as Utopia?" "Only in books, my darling," her mother said. "Only in books."

Ruffle

"Did you see the full moon last night?" Riley said. "I did,"
Byron said. "Wasn't it glorious?" she said. "It was okay,"
he said. "Look," she said, "a clown-faced woodpecker."
"Roadkill wannabes," he said. "Get a look at these
plums," Riley said, opening the bag of fruit cradled in
her lap. "Kissed by the sun." "Mm-hmm," Byron said.
"You'll feel better when we get to the beach," Riley said.
"All that sand," he said. "I want to make love to you by
the sea," Riley said. "Look," Byron said, "seagulls!"

Entrepreneurs

"Where are the Band-Aids?" Sonia said. "Mizu again?"
I said. Sonia and I run a cat hotel. Some days we host as
many as thirty cats. The cages, stacked three stories high,
come complete with all the amenities: bed, litter box,
food, water, and toys. "I can't do this anymore," Sonia
said, nursing her hand. "I'm out." "But darling," I said,
"Mrs. Baumgarten is coming to pick up Tuptim and
Pyewacket. She expects to see you." "You can tell Mrs.
Baumgarten I went to the emergency room for a tetanus
shot," she said, scooping up the car keys with her good
hand. "Where's your charming wife?" Mrs. Baumgarten
said, when she arrived. "She had to step out for a bit," I
said. "How I envy you this place," Mrs. Baumgarten said.
"Do you have a minute?" I said.

Readymade

"Are you serious?" Barry said. "Serious as taxes," Eleanor said. "What have I done?" he said. "You know very well," she said. "I have no idea," Barry said, "but if it'll make you happy, I apologize." "Go away," Eleanor said. "Darling," he said, more softly now, "you're not making any sense." "Oh, really," she said. "What's this?" "Where'd you find that?" he said. "You never used to be this careless," she said. "I think you wanted me to find it." Barry reached for Eleanor, but she pulled away. "Maybe you're right," he said, finally, "maybe it's time."

Unanimous

"Are you happy?" Therese said. "Not really," Charlie said, "Are you?" "No," she said. "We used to be happy," Charlie said. "What happened?" "I wish I knew," Therese said. "I think you'd rather live alone," Charlie said. "No," Therese said. "That's not it." "Do you still love me?" Charlie said. "Yes," Therese said. "Do you love me?" "I do," said Charlie.

III

LATE SUMMER

The air is so thick with smoke and ash right now, I
doubt I'll make it. Serves me right for dragging my heels.
When I do get to town, I buy in bulk—sacks of flour,
rice, beans; cans of creamed corn, sardines, spinach,
tomatoes. Things like that. I keep chickens, so I'm rolling
in eggs. The cat fends for herself. The wildfires will relent,
the songbirds will return, and the cat and I, for reasons
of our own, will savor the abundance.

SANDWICH

Life is complicated, right? I'll give you an example:
Today some guy almost runs me over as I'm putting
groceries in the trunk of my car. My immediate impulse
is to confront him, then I think—a miss is as good as a
mile, and what if he has a gun? I like the idea of rough
justice—but I don't want any trouble.

Covey

Two quail are steering a prodigious number of chicks
across the lawn, hastening them into the dense
undergrowth. In an instant, the quail, along with the axe
I've been grinding all morning, vanish.

A Wonderful Life

Monday, Patty broke our lunch date. Tuesday my book club disbanded. Logan called Wednesday and begged off dinner. Thursday the highway flooded, and Friday, the doorbell died. Tomorrow's Independence Day. Who doesn't love a parade?

Roots

"Did you see what they did?" Pete said. "See what who did?" I said. "They changed the name of our street—Cloverdale Avenue is now PC Boulevard." "They can't do that," I said. "It's already done," he said. We walked to the end of the block, and sure enough, the old street sign was gone. I felt like crying. "This used to be a great little town," I said. "What next," Pete said, "lavender-scented tap water? You know what *I* see when I look at a public monument? Bad art." "I worry about the whales," I said. "No matter what happens," Pete said, "I'm not moving." "Better the devil you know," I said. "It's my home," said Pete.

THE ECONOMIST

"I could have saved sixty dollars if I'd ordered that luggage myself, instead of allowing the store do it," Ella said. "Why do I do things like that?" "It's okay," I said. "Really?" she said. "Well," I said, unable to stop myself, "you may've been a bit hasty. You know how impulsive you are—especially when you want something." "Is that so?" Ella said. "If I ran every decision by you beforehand, nothing would ever get done." Sometimes, a small, seemingly insignificant misunderstanding will rattle Ella for days. During these silent storms, she'll barely look at me, let alone engage in conversation. Then, and for no discernable reason, her spirits lift, she likes me again, and life joggles on. If I were more adroit, I tell myself, I could avoid these conflicts—but no, and anyway—that's not the way it works.

Last Word

It had been a while since Jake and I had seen our old friend, Marty. He called from the road, and we made plans for lunch. During our visit we learned of his contentious divorce, his uneasy relationship with his daughter, the death of his parents, his melanoma scare, and the loss of Diego, his beloved German shepherd. Marty insisted on picking up the check. "If I leave now," he said, "I can beat the traffic." He gave us both a hug and drove off. We got home just in time for the refrigerator repairman. "Lucky for you I had a cancellation," he said. "Otherwise we'd be talking about next week." I gave Jake my *you take care of this* look, and went upstairs. "People are exhausting," I said, once the coast was clear. "Oh, they're alright," Jake said, pouring me a glass of rosé. "They mean well." "Cheers," I said.

I Forgive You

Ever since Dr. Traynor put me on a salt-free diet, I've been in a blue funk. "We're out of options," he said. In dreams, I feast on smoked salmon, marinated beef, and slabs of bacon. In fact, I do as I'm told. Yesterday, the cardiologist Dr. Traynor brought on board summoned me to her office. "Based on our analysis of your recent tests," she said, "you're going to die a very old woman." "Don't blame yourselves," I said, "you were only doing your job."

SLEEPING TIGER

I don't understand what Wanda, the new cashier at Rite Stuff, has against me. She gives me dirty looks whenever I'm there. They have everything at Rite Stuff: soda pop, panties, aspirin, hair dye, lottery tickets, alcohol, peanut butter, inner tubes, greeting cards, small appliances—everything. Today, when I handed Wanda my Senior Discount Card, she grumbled something—I couldn't hear what exactly—about "old people." I try to get along. I go out of my way to be pleasant, even when my knees are killing me. I wonder if Wanda is related to Leonard, the store manager. She certainly wasn't hired for her people skills. I wish my friend Pearl was still working at Rite Stuff. Pearl's true-blue. I've just about had it with Wanda.

CLIFFHANGER

"I'm sick of my empty, introspective life," Ivy said. "I want to live!" "What's your plan?" I said. "Sometimes I envy Patty Hearst," she said. "I think all the psychoanalysis I've had has ruined me." "Go on," I said. "What are you, a wise guy?" she said. I've been trying to get Ivy to go out with me for months, but she always turns me down. "I have swim club tonight." "I dine with my aunt every Friday." "My bird's sick." I had to make a move. "Why don't you shave your head, and hitchhike through Indonesia," I said. "Or commune with the lemurs of Madagascar." I couldn't tell if I was making any headway, but I soldiered on. "How about adventuring across Russia on the Trans-Siberian Railway," I said. Ivy shrugged. "There's a nice little Korean restaurant a couple of blocks from here," I said. "I'm starving," Ivy said.

Prodigal Son

I'm sitting in my apartment, reading a back issue of
National Geographic, when my landlord barrels through
the door. "My mother's locked in the car and I can't find
the keys!" I jump to my feet and run after him. It's barely
ten A.M., and already in the nineties. "Mom," he says,
pounding the windshield. "Open up!" I walk around to
the passenger side and peer in. "Buddy," I say, "that's
not a person in there—that's a mannequin in an old lady
wig." He takes a handkerchief from his back pocket and
mops his brow. "It's my carpool dummy," he says. "This
heat, it does strange things to a man." "Where's your
mother?" I say. "Home, I guess," he says. "I should visit
her one of these days."

The Family Jewels

"When I was your age," Grammy said, "I had more energy than I knew what to do with. Now I know what to do with it, but I don't have the energy. Bring me that box from off the credenza." I brought her the wooden box. It had always intrigued me: the delicately carved tea roses adorning the lid, the rich finish of the wood. As a child, I combed Grammy's house, in search of the key that would unlock it, my curiosity ablaze. Grammy took the box from me, cradling it in her lap. "I wish I could remember where I put the damn key," she said. "Shall I get a screwdriver?" I said. "Only if you're going to fix the lamp," she said. "Isn't that why you're here?"

Cellar Door

Samy called. She wanted me to help her look for her mother's ashes. "They're in the cellar," she said, "but I'm afraid to go down there alone." "I'll come over after work," I said. "What do you call the inverse of a vampire?" Samy said, as we descended the stairs. "I don't know," I said, "a day person?" "Haha," she said. "I need to find the exact word—it's for my thesis." "Your thesis is on vampires?" I said. "Of course not," she said. "I'm not batty." "Does this joke have a punch line?" I said. Samy hissed. "I need that noun," she said. "Is this it?" I said, indicating a small rectangular package, wrapped in blue paper and tied with string. It was laying on top of a similar package wrapped in butcher paper—no string. "That's them," Samy said. "Your folks?" I said. "Yes," she said. "Which one's your mom," I said. "I can't remember," she said, "and now it's too late."

Almost True Story

I'm calling this an almost true story because I'm writing it as if it happened to me. It didn't. It happened to my friend Angie—but she values her privacy, and a promise is a promise. Angie was walking down the street in our small Ohio town. *Sorry, Angie—I* was walking down the street in our small Ohio town, dreaming of a life that was anything but the one I'd been living. I had no idea what I wanted to do, nor did I have any particular skills, except maybe typing and a decent head for numbers. But office work depressed me. "You could be an airline stewardess," my brother suggested. I joined the Navy. Within a month they stuck me behind a desk, and for the next three and a half years, I clerked. My supervisors praised my diligence and encouraged me to re-up, but I couldn't do it. After the service, I drifted. In Baton Rouge I met a man, a honeybee keeper, who taught me the tools of the trade. I loved the work, the man proposed, and here I stand. Home sweet home.

So Close

I had a lot of fun with this one guy, a painter, but he couldn't make a living at it, and moved back to Belgium. I heard he teaches art therapy at a mental hospital and plans to marry his childhood sweetheart. There's a new man in my life. He lives in the building directly opposite mine. I like watching television when he does, and if I can tell what he's having for dinner, I'll make the same thing for myself. He eats a lot of spaghetti, then, for dessert, vanilla ice cream—straight out of the container. My dad did that. It drove my mother crazy—but I wouldn't mind.

Tailspin

I was so anxious by the time Ben came home, I could barely breathe. "You know that antique plane?" I said. "The one that's cordoned off?" he said. "That's the one," I said. "I was walking the dogs behind the airport and couldn't resist. I scooted under the barricade, stepped onto the wing, and squeezed into the cockpit. For a few magical minutes I was Amelia Earhart—that is, until the joystick came off in my hand. I shoved it back into the floor, but what if I broke something?" "The plane's a replica," Ben said. "It doesn't even have an engine." "I don't think anyone saw me," I said. "Wanna bet?" he said.

Lover Boy

I think I always knew my marriage would fail. Regina
left her husband for me and, true to type, she left me
for someone else. People don't change. These days I tell
myself I don't need anyone, but lust always gives me
away and, frankly, the prospect of besting another man
still thrills. I'm telling you all this, Sharon, because I like
you. You deserve better.

CRICKETS

The wind's been howling for days, and folks around here, especially me, are coming undone. I complain about the bathroom mirror: "Too much information!" The roads: "Long and winding!" Apples: "Not like they used to be!" It's a slippery slope. Yesterday, my next-door neighbor cut down every one of his pepper trees, while his wife stood at the window and wept. My ex has been after me all week to rid her of the cricket stuck behind her couch: "It's incessant chirping is driving me mad," she says— but when I get there, she decides to keep it. My cat stares at me as if to say, "This is all your fault." Which reminds me, there's nothing to eat.

"How do you feel?" Dr. Zhou said, when she returned to the examination room. "Same as before," I said, "except it's twenty minutes later." Dr. Zhou began removing the tiny acupuncture needles from my head, torso, and limbs. "You're not peaceful," she said. "You're telling me," I said. "I can't even imagine what peaceful feels like. Everything rattles me. Sudden noises, especially." Just then there was a knock at the door. "Sorry to interrupt," the receptionist said. "Professor Aaron is here. He says it's an emergency." "Put him in Room Two," Dr. Zhou said. "Excuse me, doctor," I said, "I think you left a needle in my neck." "Oops," she said. "It happens sometimes. Not often, but sometimes." "Do you think you can help me?" I said, swinging my legs off the table. "We're making progress already," she said. "I live in hope," I said. "Breathe," said Dr. Zhou.

More Light

Now that the gods have blinded me, I will defy them with words. Cadmium red, yellow ochre, cobalt blue, Hooker's Green. The jubilee grapes are ferruginous, the bumblebee's a wag. The wind chimes are shackled to Beethoven's Ninth, and the hummingbird's half in the bag.

Jump

It was a happy surprise when I ran into Jeremy. I hadn't seen him in ages and I missed the guy. He looked pale. "Want to grab a coffee?" I said. "I thought last Saturday was a Thursday," he said, "didn't go to work and lost my job. Fifteen years on the same corner." "You should complain to your union," I said. "There is no union for what I do," he said. "Yours is a dying art," I said. "My dream has always been to fly," he said, "but does the world really need another hot air balloonist?" I've never seen Jeremy so discouraged. "I'm supposed to clean out my locker by noon," he said. "And if you don't?" I said. "I see what you're saying," Jeremy said, the color returning to his cheeks. "I'm a free man!" "Up, up, and away," I said.

Chair

When I'm old, really old, I'm going to get a robotic chair. "Come here chair," I'll say. There'll be plenty of household robots by then—ones that talk, and smile, and say nice things, but that's a rabbit hole I'll never go down. I like the idea of a chair. There's no heartache in a chair. I'm definitely not giving the chair a name. Keep it simple, that's my motto. My goal is to have all my essentials within easy reach of the chair. I'm not lazy, quite the opposite, but I'm wearing out. Wear-out-or-rust-out I always say. Besides, once I have my chair, there'll be no stopping us.

SOLITAIRE

"I feel more connected with my loved ones when I don't speak with them than when I do," she said.

SELF RELIANCE

I need two so I buy three in case I lose one. I want to head west but it's into the sun so I'm driving north. I need directions but I'm too proud to ask. I'm hungry but too self-conscious to dine alone. I need sleep, but I can't decide where to pull over.

Pressure Drop

"Do you feel it?" Harlan said. "Feel it?" I said. "The pressure to do something," he said. "To act." "The Great Unraveling?" I said. "I'm ignoring it—and to that end, I've taken up the piccolo. It and my onion garden are my passion." "Fiddling while Rome burns," he said. "I pity you." "I have shallots, Bermudas, cipollinis, chives, Mauis, Vidalias, redwings...." "You're delusional," he said, interrupting my reverie, "and tiresome." "Wait," I said, as he made for the door. "At least try my Walla Wallas!"

Twenty four Karat

Where's Tank?" Joey said, when I bumped into him outside the deli. "He nipped the Cranston kid, who was jabbing him with a stick," I said, "and now he's in quarantine for two weeks. I feel like a ghost out here without him." "There's something wrong with that kid," Joey said. "A budding serial killer," I said. "There he is," Joey said, "bullying the little Grady girl." "Get away from her," Mrs. Grady hollered, making a beeline for the two children. She picked up the Cranston kid by the seat of his pants, held him out at arm's length, and dropped him like a stone. "Mrs. Grady's a lot stronger than she looks," I said. "I think I'm in love," said Joey.

"Come in, come in," Shelley said. He waved several handwritten pages in my direction, elbowed the basset hounds off the couch, and invited me to sit. "I'm writing a book," he said. "Listen to this...." "Unique take on childrearing," I said, when he'd finished. "Children are a waste of space," he said. "Some people like them," I said. "Those people aren't my audience," he said. "How are your folks?" I said. "Still living off the grid?" "They're in an old people's home in Tucson," he said. "They missed electricity." "At least you know where they are," I said. "Something wonderful awaits me," Shelley said, "I can feel it." "A fresh start," I said. "New horizons," he said. "Abundance," I said. We went back and forth like this until we ran out of lies and fell silent. "Do you want me to get that?" I said, when the phone rang. The dogs were hogging the couch again, and Shelley was pinned down. "Whoever it is will call back," he said. "They always do."

ACKNOWLEDGMENTS

I wish to thank Trish Reynales for her editorial elegance, and as ever, and forever, Jerry Rounds.

ABOUT THE AUTHOR

Born and raised in Los Angeles, Toni Stern enjoyed a highly productive collaboration with the singer-songwriter Carole King. Stern wrote the lyrics for several of King's songs of the late '60s and early '70s, most notably "It's Too Late" for the album *Tapestry*. The album has sold more than 25 million copies worldwide and received numerous industry awards. In 2012, *Tapestry* was honored with inclusion in the National Recording Registry to be preserved by the Library of Congress; in 2013, King played "It's Too Late" at the White House. That song, along with Stern's "Where You Lead," feature in the Broadway hit and soundtrack album *Beautiful: The Carole King Musical*. "Where You Lead" is also the theme song for the acclaimed television series *Gilmore Girls*. Stern's music has been recorded by many artists, from Gloria Estefan and Barbra Streisand to Faith Hill and Drag-On. She lives in Santa Ynez, California. *Loops* is her third volume of poetry.

A Note on the Type

Loops is typeset in Minion, designed by Robert Slimbach in 1990 for Adobe Systems. Minion was an early member of the well-regarded Adobe Originals program which featured a set of type families derived from classical styles. Minon is based specifically on typefaces, such as Jenson and Bembo, that originally appeared in Venice in the late sixteenth century—it exhibits the graceful proportions, harmonious contrast between thick and thin strokes, and sculpted serifs for which they are known. Despite its venerable origins Minion works very well for contemporary typography, and is widely used in current book design.

Made in the USA
Middletown, DE
05 May 2022